...ut I was free, and they should be free.
-Harriet Tubman

I am not afraid... I was born to do th...
-Joan of Arc

I am a queen. And as long as I live, I will reign.
-Zenobia

To create one's world in any of the arts takes courage.
-Georgia O'Keeffe

...ria Woodhull

...side of the room and the guys on the other side of the room. I guess they didn't want to associate with me. But I could hold my own with them and sometimes did better.
-Mary Golda Ross

A woman is like a tea bag. You can't tell how strong she is until you put her in hot water.
-Eleanor Roosevelt

HISTORY'S YEARBOOK

VIRGINIA LOH-HAGAN

The world has used me so unkindly. I fear it has made me suspicious of everyone.
-Mary Anning

Liberty!
–Inayat Khan's last word

If you hold your hand closed, nothing good can come in. The open hand is blessed, for it gives in abundance, even as it receives.
-Biddy Mason

GIRL ARTISTS

I've never been afraid in my life.
-Nancy Wake

I attribute my success to this: I never gave or took any excuse.
–Florence Nightingale

Women should be someone, and not something.
–Mary Cassatt

Well-behaved women seldom make history.
-Laurel Thatcher Ulrich

...ere is the day. We must welcome it with song.
–Marie Laveau

The title of Queen rang sweet to my ears.
-Catherine the Great

Contents

Introduction

We are celebrating girl artists! Artists are people who create. There are different types of art. There are visual arts. Visual arts are creative works you can see. These arts include painting and sculpting. There are performing arts. Performing arts are creative works normally done onstage. These arts include dancing, singing, and acting.

Being a girl artist hasn't always been easy. Some people have thought that women shouldn't be artists. They thought that only men could do art.

Throughout history, women have shown that they're brave. They're strong. They're creative. The girl artists in this book rise to the top. They paved the way for today's girl artists. You don't have to be famous to be an artist. Your work doesn't even have to be perfect! If you love to create and are passionate, you're an artist.

Here's to you and all the girl artists in our lives!

chapter 1

BEST ALL-AROUND

Hildegard von Bingen

> You're a world. Everything is hidden in you.
>
> –Hildegard von Bingen

The "Best All-Around" award goes to Hildegard von Bingen. Bingen lived from 1098 to 1179. She was born in Germany. She was a nun. Nuns are women who belong to a religious community. She is also a **saint**. Saints are holy people. She wrote books about science and religion. She wrote poems. She wrote music. She made art.

Her music is still popular today. She wrote over 70 church songs. She also wrote a play set to music. To her, singing was the highest form of prayer.

Bingen had visions. Visions are like dreams. She believed God was talking to her. She had paintings made of her visions. She directed the art. She had mandalas made. Mandalas are designs using shapes. They symbolize the universe.

chapter 2

MOST DETERMINED

Ruth Asawa

> I was told that it might be difficult for me ... it encouraged me to follow my interest in art.
>
> –Ruth Asawa

The "Most **Determined**" award goes to Ruth Asawa. Determined means not quitting. Asawa wanted to attend art school. But World War II happened. Asawa was **interned** during this time. Interned means to be relocated. Japanese Americans were treated unfairly. They were taken from their homes. They were sent to camps that were like jails. Families were separated. Asawa's father was separated from the family. They didn't see him for 2 years.

But she didn't quit. She studied art at the camp. She wanted to be an art teacher. But schools denied her. She kept trying. She fought for arts education. She helped create the San Francisco School of the Arts.

She's famous for her sculptures. Sculptures are art made from things like stone or wood. Asawa also made things out of wire.

chapter 3

MOST VERSATILE

Josephine Baker

> To realize our dreams, we must decide to wake up.
>
> –Josephine Baker

The "Most Versatile" award goes to Josephine Baker. Versatile means able to do many things in different ways. Baker was an African American dancer. She did many types of dancing. She's most famous for being a jazz dancer.

But she did much more. She was a spy. She worked for the French during World War II. She carried secret messages in her sheet music. She also carried secret pictures.

She adopted 12 children. The children were from different countries. She called her family the Rainbow **Tribe**. Tribes are groups.

She had many animals. She had a cheetah. The cheetah traveled with her. It slept in her bed. It rode in her car. It had a diamond collar. Baker also had a goat, pig, chimpanzee, bird, snake, and dog.

chapter 4

BEST VISIONARY

Georgia O'Keeffe

> To create one's world in any of the arts takes courage.
>
> –Georgia O'Keeffe

The "Best Visionary" award goes to Georgia O'Keeffe. A visionary is a person with clear ideas for the future. O'Keeffe was famous for painting big flowers. She painted over 2,000 works. She helped develop American **modern** art. Modern means new. O'Keeffe also helped develop **feminist** art. Feminists are people who believe women and men should be equal.

O'Keeffe also loved love. She fell in love with a photographer. She wrote many love letters to him. Some of the letters were 40 pages long. Together, they wrote over 25,000 pages to each other. They wrote often. Sometimes, they wrote 2 to 3 times a day. They did this from 1915 to 1946.

chapter 5

MOST AWARDED

Maria Tallchief

Tallchief was my name. And I was proud of it.

–Maria Tallchief

The "Most Awarded" award goes to Maria Tallchief. She was from the Osage tribe. She was America's first **prima ballerina**. Prima ballerinas are the chief ballet dancers. She was one of the few Native American ballerinas.

Tallchief struggled. People didn't want to hire her. They wanted her to change her name. Tallchief didn't listen.

She won many awards. She's in the National Women's Hall of Fame. She earned a National Medal of the Arts. She earned a Kennedy Center Honor. The Osage Nation gave her a title. The title was Princess Wa-Xthe-Thomba. This means "woman of two worlds."

chapter 6

MOST TALENTED

Clara Schumann

My imagination can picture no fairer happiness than to continue living for art. –Clara Schumann

The "Most Talented" award goes to Clara Schumann. Schumann was a German pianist. She was a great piano teacher. She wrote her own music. She played piano in **concerts** and **recitals**. Concerts and recitals are shows. Schumann changed the way people played in shows. She played from memory. She played different pieces.

She was an important female musician in the 19th century. Her father trained her from an early age. She was trained in piano, violin, and voice. She had lessons. Then she practiced 2 hours a day. She gave her first show at age 9. She played all around Europe. She was a child **prodigy**. Prodigy means a young child with great talents.

chapter 7

MOST WELL-TRAVELED

Dorothea Lange

I believe in living with the camera, and not using the camera.

–Dorothea Lange

The "Most Well-Traveled" award goes to Dorothea Lange. Lange was a famous photographer. She traveled around the world. She went to Asia. She went to South America. She went to Europe. She went to the Middle East.

Many people thought it was unsafe. They thought women shouldn't travel alone. Lange also had a **limp**. Limps are hurt legs. But this didn't stop her.

She traveled all over California. In 1936, she took a picture of a poor mother and her kids. This was her most famous photograph.

Lange received a Guggenheim Fellowship. Fellowships are given out for important short-term projects. She was offered a special job. But she refused the offer. She didn't care that it was a well-respected project. She chose to photograph interned Japanese Americans instead. She wanted to tell their stories.

chapter 8

MOST INDEPENDENT

Maria Izquierdo

> It's a crime to be born a woman ... and it's an even greater crime to be a talented woman. –Maria Izquierdo

The "Most Independent" award goes to Maria Izquierdo. Izquierdo was the first Mexican woman to show her art in the United States. This happened in 1930. Her paintings are about her Mexican culture.

Izquierdo had to grow up fast. Her father died when she was young. She lived with her grandparents and aunt. She was forced to marry at age 14. She had 3 children by age 17. She left her husband. She became a single mom.

She taught herself art. She studied art on the streets.
She went to art school. But she didn't like it. Her classmates didn't treat her well. Izquierdo also didn't like what she was learning. She chose to learn with other artists instead.

chapter 9

BIGGEST REBEL

Mary Cassatt

> Women should be someone, and not something.
>
> –Mary Cassatt

The “Biggest Rebel” award goes to Mary Cassatt. Cassatt was an American painter. She was born to a rich family in 1844. Her family wanted her to be a wife and mother. But Cassatt wanted to be an artist. Her parents wouldn’t support her. They didn’t pay for her supplies. Supplies are things needed to work. Her father said he probably would rather she die than be an artist.

Cassatt found her own way. She went to school. But the school didn’t treat her fairly. She left. She went to Europe to learn more. She went to art museums. She sold her paintings for money. She used the money to learn more. She didn’t let what others thought stop her.

chapter 10

HARDEST WORKER

Alice Guy-Blaché

Be Natural.

–Alice Guy-Blaché

The "Hardest Worker" award goes to Alice Guy-Blaché. Guy-Blaché was French. She was a filmmaker. She was a **pioneer**. Pioneers are the first people to do something. Guy-Blaché's first movie was called *The Cabbage Fairy*. This may have been the first movie to tell a story.

Guy-Blaché made over 1,000 movies. (Only 140 movies are still around.) She worked from 1896 to 1920. She directed. She wrote. She made special effects. She added sound. She even owned her own movie **studio**. Studios are like office spaces.

chapter 11

CLASS CLOWN

Fanny Brice

Let the world know you as you are, not as you think you should be.

–Fanny Brice

The "Class Clown" award goes to Fanny Brice. Brice was born in 1891. She was a comedian. Comedians are people who perform in shows and make people laugh. Brice was known as "America's first female comedy superstar." *Funny Girl* is a movie and play based on her life.

Brice could dance. She could sing. She could act. She created and starred in her own radio comedy show. The show was called *The Baby Snooks Show*. Brice acted like a baby named Snooks. Snooks was a brat. Brice performed in costume. She said, "I am Snooks. For 20 minutes or so, Fanny Brice **ceases** to exist." Ceases means stops.

chapter 12

BEST ONSTAGE PRESENCE

Bette Davis

> Attempt the impossible in order to improve your work.
>
> –Bette Davis

The "Best Onstage Presence" award goes to Bette Davis. Davis was an actor. She acted on stage. She acted in movies and TV shows. In fact, she played almost 100 different roles!

She won many acting awards. She was the highest paid woman in the United States in 1942. She played a lot of strong women.

She continued acting even when she was sick. She had breast cancer. She had a stroke. But she kept working. She worked for 60 years. She acted up until she died. She did what she loved and didn't let anything stop her.

Top Memories

- **1548:** Caterina van Hemessen was a Flemish painter. She was the first to create a self-portrait of an artist at an easel. Easels are frames that hold artists' work while they paint. Hemessen painted several female portraits. Portraits are pictures of people. She seemed to have stopped painting when she got married.

- **April 9, 1939:** Marian Anderson was a famous African American singer. She was not allowed to sing at Constitution Hall in Washington, D.C. She was denied because of her race. First Lady Eleanor Roosevelt protested. Anderson ended up singing at another concert. She sang at the Lincoln Memorial. Over 75,000 people came. When she was introduced, the announcer said, "Genius draws no color line."

- **January 30 to February 28, 1972:** Feminist art students created an art show called "Womanhouse." They used an abandoned house in Los Angeles. They made art that showed women's experiences. This show promoted feminist art.

Advice from the Field

Eva Hesse lived from 1936 to 1970. She was born in Germany. She was Jewish. She escaped from the Nazis. She moved to New York. Her mother died. Her marriage failed. Her father died. This all made Hesse very sad. She used art to help her heal. She studied art at Yale University. She became a sculptor. She made art out of strange things. Examples are wire, wax, and rubber. She died of a brain tumor. She died at a young age. She was only 34. She had doubted herself as an artist. Her mentor was Sol LeWitt. LeWitt was another artist. He advised her to stop questioning herself. He said, "Stop it and just do!" Hesse followed his advice. She also told others to trust their art. She said, "Don't ask what it means or what it refers to. Don't ask what the work is. Rather, see what the work does."

Student Life & Clubs

Are you interested in being an artist? Consider joining the Guerilla Girls. They're rebels. They're a group of women artists and art professionals. They fight discrimination. They want women and men to be treated the same. They ask, "Why haven't more women been thought of as great artists throughout history?" They wear gorilla masks. They use fake names. They use the names of famous dead female artists. They do this to focus on their message. They said, "We wanted the focus to be on the issues, not on our personalities or our own work." They make posters. They put them up in places they shouldn't. They put them up by art galleries. They put them on buildings. They share real facts on their posters. They want others to know how unfair things are. They've been all over the world. They've written books. They've been on TV. They spread their message everywhere.

"Well-behaved women seldom make history."

–Laurel Thatcher Ulrich

Did You Know...

- About 51 percent of today's visual artists are women. Studies show that they tend to earn less money than male artists.
- In the 16th to 19th centuries, women artists weren't allowed to study nude models. Nude means naked. This means they couldn't accurately draw human bodies. (Only men could do that.)
- Mariah Carey is a famous pop singer. She can sing in 5 octaves. This means that she can hit a lot of notes.

Learn More!

Amson-Bradshaw, Georgia, and Rita Petruccioli (illust.). *Amazing Artists and Designers*. Hauppage, NY: Barron's Educational Series, Inc., 2018.

Schatz, Kate, and Miriam Klein Stahl (illust.). Rad Women Worldwide: Artists and Athletes, Pirates and Punks, and *Other Revolutionaries Who Shaped History*. Berkeley: Ten Speed Press, 2016.

Simoni, Suzanne. *Fantastic Female Filmmakers*. Toronto: Second Story Press, 2008.

Your Turn!

Now, it's your turn! You get to choose the "Top of the Class: Girl Artist" winner. Who would you pick?

TOP OF THE CLASS: GIRL ARTIST

"Top of the Class" means being the best of the best. These prompts will help you think about who'd you pick for the "Top of the Class: Girl Artist" award:

- Why is this person the best "girl artist"? List reasons why this person deserves the award more than others.
- Think about how this person is different from girl artists in this book. What is special about this person?
- How is this person similar to girl artists in this book? Describe the qualities that girl artists should have. How does this person represent those qualities?
- How does this person make the world a better place? How does this person change history? Why should we remember this person?
- Girl artists often struggle. They may also face barriers. They're often told they can't do something. They don't run away when things get hard. How does this person overcome challenges?
- What type of art does this person do? What do you think about the art? How does the art move you? How does it make you feel? How does it make you think? How does it inspire you?
- Art is best when it's shared. How does this person share art?

Consider This!

TAKE A POSITION! Maya Angelou was a poet. She said, "You can't use up creativity. The more you use, the more you have." What does she mean? Argue your point with reasons and evidence.

SAY WHAT? Who is your favorite artist? Explain what this person does. Explain why this person is your favorite.

THINK ABOUT IT! Women artists aren't as well-known as men. Why is that? How does society treat male artists versus female artists? How else are women and men treated differently?

Glossary

ceases (SEES-iz) stops

concerts (KAHN-surts) shows

determined (dih-TUR-mihnd) not willing to quit

feminist (FEM-uh-nist) of the belief that men and women are equal

interned (IN-turnd) relocated, imprisoned

limp (LIMP) having a hurt leg causing a strange walk

modern (MAH-durn) new

pioneer (pye-uh-NEER) someone who helps develop or create something from the beginning

prima ballerina (PREEM-uh bah-luh-REE-nuh) the main or chief ballet dancer

prodigy (PRAH-dih-jee) a young child who shows great talent

recitals (rih-SYE-tuhlz) shows

saint (SAYNT) a very holy person

studio (STOO-dee-oh) a work space

tribe (TRIBE) a group of people that includes many families who have the same language, customs, and beliefs

Index

45th Parallel Press

Published in the United States of America by Cherry Lake Publishing
Ann Arbor, Michigan
www.cherrylakepublishing.com

Reading Adviser: Marla Conn, MS, Ed., Literacy specialist, Read-Ability, Inc.
Book Designer: Jen Wahi

Photo Credits: © Zvonimir Atletic/Shutterstock, cover (left), 4; ©FierceAbin/iStock, cover (middle), 14; ©Bain News Service, publisher/Library of Congress/Reproduction No., LC-DIG-ggbain-34089, cover (right), 24; ©Robert Clay/ Alamy Stock Photo, 6; ©cineclassico/Alamy Stock Photo, 8; ©Van Vechten, Carl, photographer/Library of Congress/ Reproduction No., LC-USZ62-103712, 10; ©Martha Holmes/The LIFE Images Collection/Getty Images, 12; ©Dorothea Lange, Resettlement Administration photographer/Library of Congress/Reproduction No., LC-DIG-fsa-8b27245, 16; ©SUN/Newscom, 18; ©Pictorial Press Ltd /Alamy Stock Photo, 20; ©Ronald Grant Archive/Mary Evans Picture Library Ltd/ age footstock, 22; ©World History Archive/Ann Ronan Collection/age footstock, 26; various art pieces throughout courtesy of Shutterstock

45th Parallel Press is an imprint of Cherry Lake Publishing.

Library of Congress Cataloging-in-Publication Data

Names: Loh-Hagan, Virginia, author.
Title: Girl artists / by Virginia Loh-Hagan.
Description: [Ann Arbor] : [Cherry Lake Publishing], [2019] | Series: History's yearbook | Audience: Grade 4 to 6. | Includes bibliographical references and index.
Identifiers: LCCN 2019004190| ISBN 9781534147881 (hardcover) | ISBN 9781534150744 (pbk.) | ISBN 9781534149311 (PDF) | ISBN 9781534152175 (hosted ebook)
Subjects: LCSH: Women artists--Biography--Juvenile literature. | Women and the arts--History--Juvenile literature.
Classification: LCC NX164.W65 L64 2019 | DDC 704/.042--dc23
LC record available at https://lccn.loc.gov/2019004190

Printed in the United States of America
Corporate Graphics

About the Author:

Dr. Virginia Loh-Hagan is an author, university professor, former classroom teacher, and curriculum designer. She plays piano, creates her own coloring pages, and makes her own cards. She also loves painting with acrylics. Her dogs are her source of inspiration. She lives in San Diego with her very tall husband and very naughty dogs. To learn more about her, visit www.virginialoh.com.